W9-CFQ-964

Chicken, Pig, Cow
and the Class Pet

Ruth Ohi

annick press
toronto + new york + vancouver

©2011 Ruth Ohi (text and illustrations)
Design: Sheryl Shapiro and Ruth Ohi

Annick Press Ltd.
All rights reserved. No part of this work covered by the copyrights hereon may be reproduced or used in any form or by any means – graphic, electronic, or mechanical – without the prior written permission of the publisher.

We acknowledge the support of the Canada Council for the Arts, the Ontario Arts Council, and the Government of Canada through the Canada Book Fund (CBF) for our publishing activities.

ONTARIO ARTS COUNCIL
CONSEIL DES ARTS DE L'ONTARIO

Cataloging in Publication

Ohi, Ruth
    Chicken, pig, cow and the class pet / Ruth Ohi.

"A Ruth Ohi picture book".
ISBN 978-1-55451-347-5 (bound).—ISBN 978-1-55451-346-8 (pbk.)

    I. Title.

PS8579.H47C446 2011   jC813'.6   C2011-900223-X

The art in this book was rendered in watercolor.
The text was typeset in Billy.

Distributed in Canada by:
Firefly Books Ltd.
66 Leek Crescent
Richmond Hill, ON
L4B 1H1

Published in the U.S.A. by:
Annick Press (U.S.) Ltd.
Distributed in the U.S.A. by:
Firefly Books (U.S.) Inc.
P.O. Box 1338
Ellicott Station
Buffalo, NY 14205

Printed in China.

Visit Annick at: www.annickpress.com
Visit Ruth Ohi at: www.ruthohi.com

For Kaarel
—R.O.

Chicken, Pig, and Cow loved best friend Dog.

Dog was brave.

Dog was helpful.

Dog always knew what to do.

But best of all, Dog
was always there for
Chicken, Pig, and Cow.

Until one day, Dog wasn't.
"Where's Dog?" asked Pig.
"Where's the ground?"
asked Chicken.

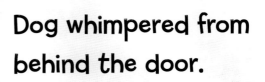

Dog whimpered from
behind the door.

Chicken, Pig, and Cow
heard noise.
Vroom.
Honk.

"Is that your stomach?"
Chicken asked Cow.
But it wasn't Cow.

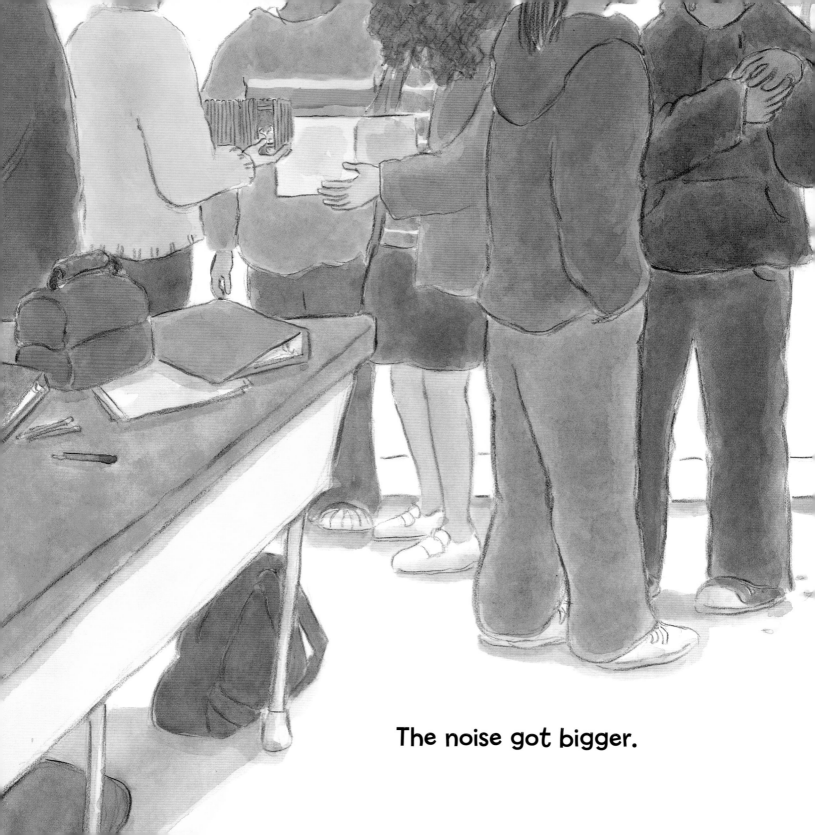

The noise got bigger.

It was school.

Faces like Girl's, but not
Girl's, peered in on them.
"It looks like a party,"
whispered Pig.
"Dog?" whispered Cow.
"We need you …"

When the faces went away,
Pig peeked out.

A furry face peeked in.

"Hello," said Cow.

Furface did not answer.

"It must be lunchtime," said Pig.

"But barns are not food!" said Chicken.

"I guess sometimes they are," said Cow.

"I am Dog," said Pig. "Grrr. Grrr."
But Furface was not afraid of Dog.

"Why doesn't he just go home?" asked Pig.
"He must belong somewhere," said Cow.

"Somewhere not eating our barn," said Chicken.

"Ta-dah!" said Pig.

"The door is so high up," said Cow.
"He must have fallen out," said Pig.
"How will he get back up?"
Chicken had an idea.

Push

Grunt

"Ta-dah," groaned Chicken.

But Furface wanted lunch.

Chicken found a better lunch.
"Tastier than a barn!"
thought Chicken.

"Fetch," said Chicken.

Whoosh

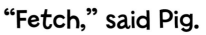

Plop

"Fetch," said Pig.

"Follow the leader," said Cow.
"I am not a salad," said Chicken.

And then Chicken, Pig, and Cow heard noise.
Lots of noise.
Girl and her friends were coming.

Pig hurried.
Chicken scurried.

And Cow

...jumped over the moon.

Teacher came to look at the barn.

"Excellent work," said Teacher.

"Very imaginative."

Chicken, Pig, and Cow beamed.

Chicken, Pig, and Cow loved their
day at school.
And when they got home, they
gave best friend Dog a full report.